My p Book

by Jane Belk Moncure
illustrated by Linda Hohag

THE CHILD'S WORLD

ELGIN, ILLINOIS 60120

Library of Congress Cataloging in Publication Data

Moncure, Jane Belk.
  My "p" book.

  (My first steps to reading)
  Rev. ed. of: My p sound box. © 1978.
  Summary: Little p fills her box with things
beginning with the letter p and they all have a parade.
    1. Children's stories, American.   [1. Alphabet]
I. Hohag, Linda. ill.   II. Moncure, Jane Belk.   My
p sound box.   III. Title.   IV. Series: Moncure, Jane
Belk.   My first steps to reading.
PZ7.M739Myp   1984   [E]   84-17553
ISBN 0-89565-288-9

Distributed by Childrens Press, 1224 West Van Buren Street,
Chicago, Illinois 60607.

My "p" Book

(Blends are included in this book.)

Little  had a box.

She said, "I will fill my  box."

Little P found a poodle

and her puppy.

"In you go," she said.

Little **p** found a pig...

and her piglets.
She put them into her box.

Then she walked to the park.

She saw a

picnic
table
and a
picnic
basket.

They were under a peach tree.

"Let's have a
picnic,"
she said.

What
a
picnic!

Little p put the
animals
back into her box.

box

She put in the leftover peanuts, pickles, popcorn, and pie too.

Now the box was so heavy, it was about to pop.

Little  P found a pony and a cart.

"Please pull us," she said.

The pony pulled them
right to a ...

porcupine.

Little P gave him popcorn.

She put him into her box.

Then she saw a peacock.

She put the peacock into her box.

Suddenly the pony stopped!

She saw a panther in the path.

The pony jumped. The animals
fell out of the box.

The panther pounced

on the box.

He ate up all the peanuts,
pickles, popcorn,
and pie.

Then a
policeman
came by.

"You have found our pet
panther," he said.

"Please help me take him back to the zoo."

piglet

porcupine

picnic basket

pony

park

piglet

piglet

pig

pupp[y]

So all the animals went to the

26

peaches

policeman

peacock

poodle

path

panther

zoo! What a parade!

More words with Little P.

pretzel

panda

pencil

parrot

PASTE

plane

pelican

parachute

puppet

plate

penguin

pocket

piano